THE FROG PRINCE
THE DARVEL EXPLORATORY SYSTEMS SHORT

S.J. SANDERS

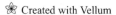 Created with Vellum

PROLOGUE

"Ms. Brody, how are you feeling?"

Gwen groaned and blinked, the lights above blinding her. As the heavy sedation wore off, the doctor's face gradually came into view. She wanted to hit something and throw up all at the same time. Her entire body ached!

"Like something ran over me," she rasped. "What did you do to me?"

He blinked down at her as she tried to recall his name. She sighed and gave up. What did it matter anyway? It wasn't like she was going to be seeing him after she got packed into the exploratory drone. The AI would be monitoring her from there on out as she made the trip to planet Xal2614 in stasis. She had been selected, and like all non-gratas who didn't enjoy the protections of planetary citizenship on United Earth, she had little real choice what Darvel did with her once she was enlisted on the exploratory division.

She just hadn't thought it would include surgery.

A hypo-syringe was pressed against her neck, delivering a wonderfully cool blast of medicine into her screaming veins. "As was explained to you, Xal2614 is a planet that, while having few oceans, has a high-water concentration over almost all of its land surfaces. Because the risk of contracting certain illnesses was high, we decided to do a wide range of genetic modifications in addition to surgical implants that had already been approved for initial exploratory recruits."

She shook her head. "What does that mean?"

He smiled down at her patiently and patted her arm. She blinked at the strange feel of his hand on her skin. It felt muffled slightly and like his hand just slid off of her. *Weird.*

"Because the initial exploratory recruits are never retrieved and are left to survive on their own as they collect data until the first colonization ships arrive—if the planet is green-lighted for colonization—it has made it necessary to consider alterations for human adaptability on the planet with colony equipment and support. It is an expensive and complicated procedure but one well worth the wait. Although you have been in recovery for a month in a medically induced coma while you recovered from the surgery, we were able to do successful skin grafts and a few internal organ transplants as we modified you on a genetic level to be compatible with an amphibious life."

She gaped up at him in shocked horror, afraid to even look down at her body. He squinted down at her with delight. "Don't look so worried, dear. It was a perfectly logical solution. You see, we all, after all, have an amphibious stage in development. We merely recoded your genes to accept our necessary alterations and to make it so that they will also impact any offspring you have with..." He glanced at his data-pad. "... Christopher Evans, the other recruit being sent down."

He looked back up at her, his eyes crinkling. "Darvel also decided to green-light reproductive license for recruits in the hope of getting longer lasting data collection that can extend beyond the lifetime of the initial recruits. Breeding with Mr. Evans is thereby a part of your mission as well."

She shook her head in denial. This couldn't be right. This had to be illegal. The Darvel Board Commission was insane! Her arm shot up revealing a slick, pebbly green flesh that ran down the entire visible length, down to black, claw-like nails and a pale-yellow webbing between her fingers. Her scream bubbled out of her just as another hypo-needle hit her neck, sending the world hazy.

"Just rest now, Ms. Brody. When you wake up you will be on Xal2614 and will be feeling much better."

The world slowly disappeared into blackness and Gwen's last conscious thought was that she highly doubted that she would be feeling better at all.

CHAPTER 1

$\mathcal{F}$uck, who the hell turned on the overhead brights? Gwen stretched her legs as she brought a hand up to shield her face, ready to murder her cabinmate. Their small shelter on Xal2614 was cramped with barely enough space for either of them to turn around and zero privacy. She supposed that was an intentional design considering that they were supposed to… breed. She grimaced and kicked off the light blanket covering her.

At least Chris was giving her as much space as possible and wasn't trying very hard to get into her pants. Not yet anyway. The subject came up a few times since they awakened from stasis in their travel pod though she'd had a few days of reprieve as they worked to set up the shelter from the supplies that had been jettisoned to the planet with them.

But after that. The day-to-day monotony as they began to record the minute observations had led to an increasing awareness of the way Chris's gaze seemed to linger on her. It was disconcerting but he was still acting like a gentleman and giving her space. She knew it was only a matter of time before it came up again. How exactly did one tell someone that they had no intention of ever sleeping with them if they can avoid it? It wasn't that she held anything against him but there was zero attraction on her part and, frankly, Darvel's expectations just rubbed her the wrong way.

Forced breeding had not been in the informational docket that she had received. In fact, she was pretty sure it was very illegal. Non-gratas may not enjoy all the privileges of citizens but they still had basic human rights and protections. Didn't they?

She glanced down at her skin and cringed and the splotched color from the skin grafts. It was a reminder that Darvel had moved far away from United Earth's legalities. All of this had been done on a station deep in space, after all. Who would even know back on Earth what had happened to her? It certainly wasn't like she could complain about it. She would never see Earth again, that much was clear. Worse was that, though the genetic alterations they made on her allowed her body to accept the changes the scientists wrought, she would never get used to it. The emerald and hints of teal with golden yellow webbing between her fingers and toes might have been pretty if it wasn't for the fact that it was on her.

She couldn't change what they did to her but she sure as hell wasn't going to go along with their plans and fuck some man she barely knew and wasn't attracted to in order to spawn offspring for Darvel. Fuck that and fuck them.

Speaking of, where was Chris anyway?

Pulling on a simple, body-hugging jumpsuit designed especially for their new environment, Gwen padded out from the single bedroom that had been graciously left to her into the main room of their living pod and glanced around. The cushioned sitting bench where he slept was pristine, the blanket folded up and left on one corner and the kitchen that adjoined the space was empty. Usually, he had coffee brewing since he was more of a coffee addict than she was.

"Chris?"

Silence met her and Gwen frowned. Did he step outside? They had a rule between them that no one went outside alone. It was a strange world and neither of them knew what sort of dangers were out there that they were not yet aware of.

She placed her palm on the lock pad beside the door and waited for it to register her signature. The door whooshed open, and she stared out at the swamp on the other side, the water creeping up around the dock that they had painstakingly built around their habitation pod. The swamp itself, she had mixed feelings about. It was beautiful with giant blossoms on stalks and thick reedy plants with broad leaves interspersed among gigantic, towering trees with enormous roots rising above the waterline. It was completely alien and yet, in some ways, how she imagined Earth might have been when the superior life forms had been dinosaurs.

A giant beetle-like insect with long dragonfly wings zipped by and Gwen jumped despite being safely inside the shelter. She swallowed and peered around. Other than the sudden appearance of the bug, everything was unnervingly silent, the thick mist that drifted among the trees, obscuring the planet from the satellite that had been established in this solar system.

"Chris?" she whispered. "This is not funny. If you are trying to scare me, quit. I told you that I don't celebrate Halloween."

He had been obnoxiously elated yesterday that it was October and had gone on and on about all the creepy ways he had cele- brated the holiday growing up. Gwen didn't get it. Sure, she did trick or treating in the restricted areas for non-gratas as a kid, but she had never enjoyed being scared and that was exactly what it was all about once one became a certain age. All the creeps and chills she could do well without.

A strange pulsing, rhythmic song rose up, the eerie, hollow notes sending a chill down her spine despite their beauty.

"And this is how every horror movie begins, with some creepy ass soundtrack to lure you in. I have seen a horror movie or two in my life and am not so stupid that I'll come out there, Chris, so you can stop with the theatrics. Put away whatever you found to make that sound, and come inside. I'll get coffee going."

Silence. Whatever it was stopped. She shivered, wrapping her arms around her middle, waiting for Chris to pop out from behind one of the large trees. But he didn't. There was no sound except a soft splashing that had her head snapping around in an attempt to locate the source of the sound.

She jumped as the pulsing notes started again... closer.

"Please, stop," she begged, her voice wobbling as fear crawled up into throat.

It stopped and she could have cried out with relief except that a large splash broke the silence, and she spun around, half-furious and ready to chew Chris out for trying to scare her. He would be laughing at her, she was certain.

The words died on her tongue as her eyes met the amber-orange stare of something peering up at her from the water. Her tongue glued to the top of her mouth and a tremor ran through her. It wasn't Chris. It was nothing recognizably human, not even with their own altered features. The face was a deep violet that seemed to shift in hues of blue and purple with colorful yellow and orange bumps visible on its forehead and just under its eyes. And it didn't have human hair. In place of hair, there were long rubbery strings braided across the top of its head and floating in the water around it. Two sets of eyelids blinked, and it shifted closer.

Gwen squealed and stepped back, slamming her hand on the pad to initiate the door-lock. The door whooshed closed as she stumbled back further into the house. She stood there in the middle of the living room, her hand pressed against her chest, feeling her heart race under her palm. No sound came from the other side of the door, no sound on the dock and no collision against the door. Slowly she crept toward the viewing screen that showed perimeter views around the habitation pod. With a flick of her fingers, she magnified the one in front of her house, drawing it up to the fore of the screen.

She shuddered. There it was. Whatever it was, it was still out there.

It seemed to peer right back at her as it drew back slightly from the dock and rose further from the water. She froze. Its features looked almost human. Possessing a strong jaw and a vaguely humanoid nose though less pronounced and more of a thick ridge on its face with a pair of slit nostrils at the end, it looked like a better and more natural version of whatever she and Chris were supposed to be. Even its ears were similar except that they were longer and pointed, the webbed ends crinkling back. More of that strange textured skin covered is throat and muscled chest, the spray of color yellow and green bumps marking it like constellations. More importantly, however, it wore a necklace made of glowing stones and what appeared to be frighteningly large predatory teeth. Its head cocked as it stared back at her—or rather at her door—and then its throat swelled, turning a pale purple—as the pulsing song, not unlike frog song now that she felt safe enough to listen closer—issued from it.

It didn't approach but it didn't leave either. More worrying, there was no sign of Chris. Had that thing killed him the moment he stepped outside? Hours passed, the light shifting over the swamp marking the passage of hours until finally it dimmed and darkened as night fell and still no sign from Chris, nor could she hail his comm with the comm system's broadcaster.

Shivering, she dropped onto the couch and stared at the frog alien who had settled on a nearby root. Black pants covered its lower body and looped with stirrups around feet with long, webbed toes. It had pulled on gloves over its clawed, webbed hand that seemed to protect the webbing as it foraged around. She wondered if the webbing between the fingers was more sensitive and easier to damage since it did not take the same care with its feet that were similarly clawed.

As the swamp darkened, its colorful splotches became luminescent and its amber eyes glowed, cutting through the dark so that she was able to see clearly where it was. Other than climb around the nearest tree, it didn't venture any closer but nor did it leave. It stayed right where it was... watching her. And she watched it in turn until sleep finally claimed her.

CHAPTER 2

*I*t was still out there. Still watching her. She didn't know what it wanted, but whatever it was, it didn't seem that it was interested in attacking. Or at least it was making no attempt to get into the habitation pod. Nor was it attempt to lure her out unless its creepy singing was meant to do so.

It wasn't, right?

She frowned and pressed her hand against her belly. She had awoken to its singing and the sound had sent heat spikes deep into her ever since, the sensation dropping to a low smolder whenever the singing ceased. It was strange. It had not affected her that way yesterday.

Fuck, please don't be a side-effect of the changes to my biology.

Amid all of that there had been song-like vocalizations that had recently started just a few hours ago that her translator was rapidly beginning to process. Now she was catching occasional words that were entirely random without context and one word in particular that didn't have translation but stood out among them as often as it was repeated. Jymlina.

What was a jymlina?

Where. Hold. Sing. The barrage of words were maddening, called out at a volume that she couldn't hope to ignore them as the translator provided more and more words.

And still Chris had not returned. At this point, she might as well count him as dead. They never stayed away from the habitat overnight. There were predators that hunted the swamp. At night they could hear the screams and cries of the wildlife. He never would have stayed out there unless he was unable to return. She was caught between fear that she was now alone out there, regret for his death, and the arousal that was slowly crawling through her as the heat expanded from her belly with an acute lust that her skin crawled with it.

Had the scientists known that this would happen? She snorted mirthlessly. Oh, she had no doubt. They had probably banked on him figuring out how to trigger her instinct in this way. Now that she thought back on it, sometimes she heard him making similar, disjointed notes that she figured were due to the amphibian characteristics given to them. It hadn't sounded as beautiful as the song being sung by the alien, but now that she thought about it, she could make the correlation.

She scratched an itchy spot behind her ear in annoyance. She was going to need to slather on more moisturizer. Her skin produced a natural protective mucus, but the scientists had them strip it daily so that their data signatures were clear. It was a painful process that left her skin exposed and constantly itchy. There were times when it got really bad that she was tempted to just burrow into the muddy water out there and soak it in. The moisturizer was the only thing that brought her relief. At least it was a small distraction from the arousal tormenting her.

What was it about frogs... there was something teasing her memory, something about the evolution of the frogs in cities that sprawled across Earth and how it affected their songs that felt relevant to her situation.

With a grunt of impatience, she went to the data system and typed in her query. As usual, she was forced to wait several minutes for the system to make contact with the wandering satellite, but finally it went through. She read it over, her mouth pinching. That was what it was. The evolution of the frog song. Though there were preserves, those areas that were populated had few areas that were set aside to support natural wildlife. The frogs were one of the few things that survived there. And without many natural predators there, the songs had shown marked complexity during mating season, drawing the female to them.

Was her amphibian and mammalian DNA cocktail doing this to her? Instead of simply drawing her, it was triggering what felt like a heat cooking inside of her, demanding satisfaction. To be bred.

If this was intentional… well then Darvel certainly got the last laugh on her. She wouldn't have been able to resist Chris once he worked out how to sing.

Gwen leaned back in her chair and rubbed her eyes with her hands, a small laugh bubbling out of her. What were the chances that somehow Darvel had been too clever for its own good and accidentally made her compatible with an amphibian-like species native to this planet. Oh, it wouldn't have been done intentionally. Darvel was dead set against cross species mating since it divided loyalties, though purists on Earth were told that it was to preserve the human uniqueness within the galaxy.

What an ironic twist. She was going to be plagued with a need to breed whether it came from Chris or not. But Darvel was going to hate plan B. Her shoulders shook with laughter, her eyes streaming. Her ability to resist may wane away, but at least she will be the one to have the last laugh after all and stick it to the Corp.

Where. Found. Come out.

She blinked at the entreaty. That was the first two words that the translator actually managed to string together.

Come out, jymlina.

She shivered as the song picked up again. *Okay, scratch that. He's definitely trying to lure me.*

She was just guessing here at the alien's sex based on her reactions. He had struck her as male when she first caught sight of his muscular form, but she knew that didn't mean anything. The fact that she was being aroused right now was more the deciding factor. As far as she knew, women never inspired that reaction in her, but these were aliens, and her body was quite different now. She really couldn't depend entirely on any of her assumptions.

"Female, do not be shy."

A whole sentence now. It seemed that the alien was getting chatty if the translator was being given to speed up the translation possible. More than that, his voice sounded closer. Way too close.

It went on for hours, her translator picking up more and more until his voice was coming in clear, the learned data stored in her memory center. She touched a finger to her throat implant that allowed her to vary her vocal sounds beyond the normal human ones. She could communicate with him theoretically—if she wanted.

Rubbing her arms, Gwen quickly walked back over to the view screen where she kept the fore camera open. Her eyes widened. Though the sun was beginning to sink, it was still bright enough for her to see that he was right there on her dock, his brows dropped in an expression of frustration. He paced back and forth, his head tipping back as he examined her habitation pod.

"Your male is gone," he said casually, his eyes dropping back down to peer at the door—and consequently at her. His nostrils flared. "His song did not put you in need, mine did."

His eyes hooded, the amber gleaming, and he smiled displaying a mouth full of sharp teeth with elongated canines. She

14

wished that the sight of them cooled the heat coursing through her, but to her shame it did not.

"Do you not feel it?" he said, his hollow voice dancing along her nerves making her shiver with longing. "How long I have waited for a female to call for me, for her instincts to choose my song above all others. You are mine, princess. You will not be able to wait in there forever."

Her lip curled at the arrogance. Storming to the door, she screamed through it, the inhuman sounds falling from her lips, though it lacked the precise hollow quality that his possessed.

"You are insane! Go away!"

"As you wish, jymlina."

He chuckled and she heard a splash. Hurrying back over the viewscreen, she watched as he swam back to the tree facing the habitat pod and pulled himself back onto its large roots, water streaming from his body and form-fitting pants that clung to his legs like a second skin, leaving little to imagination when it came to the sculpted muscle of his legs and ass.

She turned away, refusing to look at him longer and busied herself with preparing dinner, her belly knotting as his song began again.

Chris was gone for certain now, but what exactly did that mean. And did that creature kill him? She shivered at the unknown and forced a bite of food into her mouth. One thing was for sure, the heat was getting worse. The alien was right. She wouldn't be able to hold out forever, something she became aware of with every passing hour. Her sex was swollen and wet with arousal, her nipples taut and aching. The ache was driving deeper, making her belly spasm lightly but the cramps were getting stronger.

This wasn't good. It wasn't good at all.

CHAPTER 3

*G*wen rubbed her body needily against her bedding, her supersensitive skin sending pleasure rolling through her, increasing her arousal. She had to get up. She had duties to see to, though she didn't look forward to stripping her skin, but Darvel would be waiting for the verification. How much longer would she be able to keep it up if she was getting worse by the hour?

This was all the damned alien's fault. Maybe if she talked to him and explained—if he saw that she was not the same species as him—the alien would understand and go away. If he was gone there was perhaps some chance that she would go back to normal.

What drew him there, anyway? What had she done differently before he arrived? She frowned. Their routine had been the same as always—except one thing. Her eyes widened. She had released a small probe in the water off the dock just the other day. Darvel had required readouts from the swamp water, something that they had delayed providing in case the signal attracted predators in the water to them. They had known that they wouldn't be able to put it off forever but now she wished that they had refused the direct command from Corp. It was too much of a coincidence that the very next day Chris went missing and the alien appeared practically at the dock.

Perhaps Corp would have a suggestion on how to repel the alien, considering it was their technology that drew him. She would try that before she risked her neck trying to communicate with the strange male lurking outside.

But first... she needed to strip her skin. If she was going to be on comm, she needed to show that she was adhering to orders as close as possible when she reported Chris's absence and the presence of the alien.

Stepping into the cleansing stall, she pressed the nob that started up the pump that drew water from beneath the habitat and filtered it, adding chemicals to score the surface of her skin. Though she braced herself, the contact of the water conditioned with stripping solution made her scream as it ran over her, spraying her thoroughly from all directions. It always was uncomfortable but now it sent agony through her over-sensitized skin. She felt like her skin was blistering under it. Her clawed fingers scraped against the walls of the unit, tears streaming down her face, as she counted with the flashes of the running unit.

The pulsing light died, and the water trickled to a stop, leaving Gwen gasping for pained breaths. Her limbs shaking, she stumbled out of the stall and grabbed the towel. She dabbed at her skin, unable to stand the excruciating agony. Her normally—as normal as it could get—green and teal skin was streaked an angry red. Biting back a muffled sound of pain, she bit her bottom lip as she dropped the towel and reached for the moisturizing cream. Its coolness barely soothed her irritated skin. Thankfully, it wasn't blistered as it had felt.

Setting the cream down, she stared at her nude reflection. She looked a lot like the alien so far as texture went. She had fewer bumps on her skin, and they were tiny like pearls but none of them colorful or bioluminescent like his were. Her eyes didn't glow either, the light blue-green the same as she always had. Aside from her skin, her appearance was wholly human, and out of place on features that had suited the alien so well. Even her hair looked out of place in comparison to his rubbery crest of tendrils that covered his head. She looked like the scientist project she felt like, right down to the scars that ran down the length of her body from her skin grafts that didn't quite fade all the way.

Turning away from the mirror, she entered her sleeping quarters again and dug out a clean jumpsuit, dragging the water-repelling material over her body. Once she was sure that she was presentable, she walked through the common room, ignoring the viewscreen entirely, and made her way to the room at the other end of the habitat where the comm unit was set up. Pulling out the seat, she dropped down into it and initiated contact.

Corp's insignia rotated slowly on the screen as the system hooked into the satellite to broadcast the single across star systems until connection was made to Darvel's space station. She stiffened as the familiar face of her project commander, Nicholas Varis, filled the screen; his brows drawn into a heavy scowl.

"What is the meaning of this Ms. Brody? You are not due to report for another week."

Gwen shifted nervously in her chair and cleared her throat. The man was intimidating. Wearing a pressed suit that cost more money than she ever saw in a month and a no-nonsense haircut, he was the picture of authority as his eyes bore into her.

"Yes sir, I understand that. There have been complications."

His eyes narrowed. "Explain. And what is wrong with your skin? Are you having an allergic reaction to something down there incompatible with human physiology? As you understand, we left as much of your metabolism as human as possible. It would do us little good to have you down there if you were unaffected by things that would kill us."

She swallowed. "Nothing like that but my skin... condition... is part of what I need to report."

"Well go on then," he interrupted impatiently.

Drawing in a steadying breath, she spat out the facts as quickly and coherently as possible. As she gave her report, however, his expression steadily grew from annoyed to furious. With a slash of his hand, he cut her off as she was telling him about the alien was trying to lure her out and turned to hit his comm.

"Tell Dr. Merel to get his ass up here... now."

Turning back toward her, Varis folded his hands on the desk in front of him. He did not say a word, simply stared stonily at her. When she tried to speak to finish her report, he held up a hand, effectively silencing her. After several minutes the one man she hated more than anyone in existence hurried into the room, adjusting his labcoat. He gave her a curious glance as he dropped down into a chair that he pulled up the side of the desk. Varis nodded to him in greeting before finally addressing her.

"Now, Miss Brody, I will need you to repeat everything you just told me to Dr. Merel."

"I may need to interrupt to ask questions," the scientist broke in and Varis inclined his head in agreement.

"Now proceed," Varis grumbled as he sat back in his chair, his eyebrows beetled low of her eyes.

With a nod, she started from the beginning, starting with the probe that they had dropped the other day and her suspicion that it had led to the events that unfolded. The scientist's expression became more concerned as she spoke, his eyes shifting warily to the project commander at his side when she got to Chris's disappearance and the arrival of the alien who bore startling similarities to their hybrid form, and her own body's inexplicable reaction to him.

"Well," Varis growled, cutting Merel a fierce glare, "what do you have to say to *that*. You assured me that there would be no problems with adjusting them on a genetic level. We don't need a repeat of Turongal, damn it!"

Merel gaped, his mouth opening and closing wordlessly for several minutes, and shook his head. "This shouldn't be possible. We took every precaution using genetic material sourced only from Earth amphibians. There shouldn't be biological compatibility. In fact, using the amphibian codes should have greatly reduced the chances of it happening. There was a one in a million probability of this happening. It was such a small chance that we considered it beyond even worrying about. You saw the numbers yourself."

"Okay, but it's happened," Gwen interjected, hoping to head off the argument she could see coming. If they wanted to have a blow out over the research, they could do it without her. "What I want to know is, if the probe perhaps drew them here, is there a signal that could perhaps drive them away?"

Merel's mouth pinched thoughtfully. "You said they are bioluminescent? It is possible that they put out biological pulses, similar to the song you heard, if it is tied to mating. Hormone levels might put out a different pulse identifying a female—like fireflies firing off, distinguishing the males from the females. In a swampy, fog covered world, it is probably the way they have evolved to locate suitable mates. It is possible that the pulse of the signal identifies the probe as female." His mouth curved humorlessly. "Which explains why it is has shifted position by several yards. Your suitor likely tracked the pulse to the spherical transponder."

"Probably discarded it in a fit realizing it wasn't the real thing," Varis muttered. Sighing he pinched the bridge of his nose. "So, we have an amorous frog who is now swimming around the habitat and who may have killed Mr. Evans as a perceived rival.

The question is, can we deliver a different pulse to frighten him away long enough to retrieve Ms. Brody?"

"You can't be considering a retrieval!" Merel protested. "The data we've been getting in—"

"Is irrelevant," Varis snapped. "You assured me that the drones picked up no signs of intelligent life and now this. We are already under scrutiny for hiding evidence of alien life, we cannot afford another inquiry from the Intergalactic Coalition. The only way we can salvage this is by retrieving our asset, although, do not mistake me, Dr. Merel, I will be advising the Board to not go ahead with any further genetic modifications until we work out exactly what happened here. Hopefully Ms. Brody's biological reactions will give us valuable information. Regardless, we have too much money dumped into Ms. Brody to simply leave her there. We can put her into stasis afterwards until we find another assignment or use for her."

Stasis. They meant to retrieve her and put her to sleep—for how long? Her skin crawled at the implication. She would have not even the small pleasures she enjoyed as a non-gratas. They were going to just stick her in a freezer and forget about her until they happened to need her again. Her blood chilled at his callous words. Another use for her.

Varis leaned forward as he addressed her. "Stay inside the habitat. Do not engage with the alien species. Your med kit is equipped with several doses of tranquilizer. I will send you the codes needed to initiate the emergency stasis pod within your bedframe. Hold for transmission."

The comm system flashed, a string of numbers scrawling across it.

"Get yourself safe, Ms. Brody and we will see you in a month's time."

The comm screen blinked out, Varis's face replaced once more with the Corp's insignia. She stared at it blankly, hardly able to believe it. They were treating her like a thing… like property. All non-gratas knew that their lives were expendable, but they were still treated like human beings. She wouldn't even have that anymore. She was an asset—property of the corporation—and nothing more. She wasn't going to be able to stay there, not if she wanted any sort of life. She had a month to work out what she was going to do.

Standing on shaky legs, Gwen stepped away from the comm system and walked slowly into the common room. She hesitated only a moment before walking over to the door and placing her hand on the lockpad. The door retracted and she stared into the swamps, her throat closing at the sight that greeted her. Dozens of glowing eyes peered at her, their songs initiating and floating up from the swamp at the sight of her.

What the fuck!

Her eyes snapped to the tree where her visitor had spent the last couple of days. He was still there, his eyes sweeping over the crowd of aliens with a threatening glower. His throat turned lavender but not as pale as it did when he sang, and it didn't observably swell from what she could see at her distance. It didn't need to. He didn't sing. Instead, a sharp, hissing shriek escaped him, the note long and drawn out, rendering the other aliens silent. But only for a moment. Within short order they all started again, and Gwen slammed the door in a panic.

Oh hell no! She didn't do group sex. She was going to have to escape from the roof and hope that no one thought to look to the trees. Hopefully their climbing skills were poorer than her own.

CHAPTER 4

hey weren't leaving, and the first was getting pissed. His hissing had grown worse throughout the next day as she had hunkered down inside the habitat pod after packing necessary supplies for an extended exploration further from base and waited, hoping that the crowd would eventually lose interest and disperse. No such luck.

Now she merely waited for nightfall. Unlike them, she did not have markings that would reveal her presence in the night. Not even her high-tech night vision goggles dispelled visible light. Whereas everything gave away their presence, she would be able to stealthily move above them. She just needed to do something about masking her scent as much as possible.

Tearing through the lab that was connected by a hall off of the common room, Gwen picked up a bottle. Lilotu, she called it, with an idea of perhaps appealing to manufacturers as a new perfume that not only smelled wonderfully with a pleasing floral scent that reminded her of gardenias, but also repelled biting insects effectively. Even better, it had a heavy scent that was certain to work. The oil wasn't thinned out at all from the concentrated extraction she had made of one of the giant flowers she had found fallen near their habitat. One bloom was all it took to make a full bottle of potent extraction. Even after weeks of both her and Chris using it, it hadn't even made a dent in the bottle. It was a pity that it was a resource that no one else would ever see the benefits of because, even if they retrieved the habitat pod, the oil was coming with her.

Hastily she slapped it on, covering herself thoroughly with its overpowering scent, and carefully tucked the bottle into her pack. Drawing the straps of the bag over her shoulders she walked quietly around the habitat making the final preparations for her departure. The very last thing she did, however, was send out a lengthy comm transmission to the receiving department for the Intergalactic Coalition. Corp would be pissed but she didn't care. There was nothing more that they could do to her.

But now it was time to go.

Returning to the common room, she pulled the bench away from the wall into the center of the room and knocked its cushions onto the floor. Once it was bared, she promptly climbed on and stretched her arms toward the emergency hatch at the top. Though it was built just in case the area flooded and they would need to escape quickly, it now made for a convenient escape. The hatch didn't give easily, but it slowly lifted under force before popping up the rest of the way, giving her more than enough room to scurry out. Gripping the edge, she pulled herself up with a grunt. Thank goodness she had weeks of climbing all over this part of the swamp because that move wouldn't have been possible if she had attempted it before. She had never been particularly athletic, and her body reminded her of the fact as she sat on the roof and quietly panted.

The males were still singing and hissing at the front of the habitat, so she slipped further toward the back until she was just over the lab. Quickly, she scrabbled onto the nearest tree, swinging herself up onto one of the thick limbs overhanging the roof before hurrying among the thick, interwoven branches from tree to tree in the opposite direction from her collection of unwanted suitors.

Hurrying, of course, was a relative term since she often crept and stumbled, grabbing ahold of other branches above her or the long reeds growing high in the air from the water as she navigated her way above the swamp. But she was steadily putting distance between herself and the habitat and that was what mattered the most.

The sun was creeping over the trees when she finally stopped to rest. Leaning against the huge expanse of the tree, she settled on the wide branch with a weary yawn. She hadn't heard any of the "frog song" from the aliens for hours now. She had earned her rest as far as she was concerned. She would close her eyes just for a moment.

It was a soft tap on her arm and a long note drawn through the air that roused her. She jerked upright, her pulse hammering and blinking against the midday sun. A pair of long, muscular legs dropped in front of her before being followed by a familiar violet torso as the alien lowered himself down from the branch above her. His clawed toes touched the deep green branch first, but he lowered himself into a crouch until he was straddling her smaller body beneath his. Amber eyes met hers at a disconcertingly proximity.

Had he been up there above her head the entire time? She nearly choked back a laugh as a crazy thought came to her. He was her very own frog prince. Her mother had read the story long ago when she had been very young, but she recalled that there was a golden ball, and a maiden and frog who met at the water's edge. The frog had slept on her pillow and sat on her lap. The difference was, she wasn't a princess, no matter what the alien called her, and she was pretty sure he wasn't going to turn into a human.

But, then again, could she really be counted as human anymore? It seemed that Corp didn't consider her such.

She swallowed nervously as he sang another couple of notes, but she didn't need it. The heat had been tolerable when she was exerting herself and focusing on her getaway but the moment that she woke it raged through her, twisting her belly with the intensity of her need.

"Stop," she hissed as she attempted to lift her legs to kick him away.

He peered down at her, unimpressed with her pathetic attempt to dislodge him and crouched down lower so that his thighs brushed hers, as did a hard bulge where she suspected cock was hidden if his biology shared any further similarities to humans.

"Why do you fight?" he replied. A long, fingerless gloved hand extended toward her face so that his claws traced lightly against her cheek. "You only hurt yourself, jymlina."

"What... what is jymlina?" The words came out in a sharp pant, a tightening sensation flooding her pussy as it flooded with a hot, wet rush of desire.

His head tipped, his mouth curving at her response. "It is the sweetest of flowers. Your scent reminds me of it, though it is faint now beneath the perfume of the hundred year old lopopus bloom."

She grimaced. It seemed that her admirer had managed to track her scent after all. But if he could... Gwen looked around apprehensively until a surprisingly warm hand touched her knee. More than warm, it ran hotter than human temperature through her skin so that it was a pleasant temperature that made her want to curl into it.

"They are not there. The other males did not have days to become accustomed to your sweet scent. I could track it anywhere," he crooned as he leaned in and brushed his cheek against her own. He sniffed at her and made a trilling sound that seemed to communicate pleasure. "So familiar and yet so different."

"Because I'm not like you. I'm of another species altered to survive here. Since we are getting a little too familiar here—who and what are you?"

A look of amusement flitted across his face, though she was uncertain of the reason. Did he find their situation funny or the fact that she was disconcerted with their proximity.

"Zyr Garlorthal Warderoon Bia. Clan prince and your mate." She really wanted to strenuously object to that last part, but he continued on as if he wasn't just pronouncing her fate as if it were fact. "You are in the Warderoon clan lands that stretch from the Zungolee River to the Aprachen Mountains."

She paused. There were mountains on this planet? Why the fuck weren't they landed there instead of the middle of a swamp? Then again, Corp admitted that their readings through the dense fog were conflicting, telling them little other than the fact that there was a largely watery terrain. She shook her head. *Focus Gwen. That's not important right now.*

"Ok… Prince Zyr Gar—"

"Zyr," he interrupted with a smile. She focused on it, noting that his mouth was slightly wider than that of a human, perhaps to accommodate all those sharp teeth, with full lips. "There is no need for formality among mates."

Wow, he is persistent. She drew in a deep breath, trying to think beyond her surging hormones and the intense heat rushing through her body. "I can appreciate that you believe that, but we are not. Believe me. Humans don't work that way. Regardless of how I've been changed to adapt to this world, I'm human and I know that what I'm feeling is not real for me. Neither is whatever you think you feel for me."

He chuckled, his laughter containing a light trill that ran through it though it was deep and lovely in its resonance. "The only thing that is real, is this. This is all that matters. You say it is not real when you are twisting beneath me, your body calling for mine?"

She froze, embarrassment inching through her. He was right. She was practically grinding against him and hadn't even realized it, his pelvis brushing hers with every arch of her hips.

"But we are not the same," she protested, grasping at anything that might make him see reason even when a tiny part of her brain wondered why she was trying so hard to convince him. "You can't want to do this... not really."

She shouldn't want him like she did. It was not only against United Earth's law but she had never even entertained the thought of being with an alien. She hadn't even indulged in black market Aturian videos that her friends giggled over. So why did she want him to touch her and why was she so desperate with a need to be fucked but him repeatedly until she can't move?

"You are different," he acknowledged. "But it is appealing. I would find much pleasure with you as my mate. Even your coloring is unlike ours, brighter, and that too is fascinating."

He clearly wasn't about to be dissuaded and, try as she might, she couldn't deny that she found his differences appealing as well. Too appealing.

She groaned as another hot spasm passed through her, her pussy drenching with another hot flood of arousal. His hand brushed her hair tenderly.

"Allow me to ease you," he whispered. "You are in need, and it pains me to see you suffer needlessly."

It didn't sound like a line when there was a genuine note of concern in his voice. It was sweet, and that frustrated her, making it harder for her to reject his advance. Even Chris, though he had been friendly, had never taken her own needs into consideration when he had attempted to talk her into sex. It had been all about the assignment and working off stress. Why couldn't Zyr act like an arrogant ass so that it would be easier to push him away.

Gwen shot him an impatient look. "I'm not going to be tied for life to someone I don't know just because of a biological imperative," she snapped.

"You wish to breed without mating?" His brows raised in surprise as if shocked by the suggestion. "It is unheard of. No female would permit a male disgrace her in such a way as not to tie her to him first."

"Yeah, well, call it a human thing," she grumbled, tightening her arm around the ache in her belly, hoping that the pressure might mute the feeling further. "I prefer to actually know the male I'm shackling myself to first."

He gave her a doubtful look. "The rise to the song always tells true. I sang and you responded. You would not have if you were not the one, but if you wish to be convinced, then I shall oblige," his hissed as he flattened his body against hers, the heat of his body pouring into her.

The lust that had been burning within her exploded in a frenzy of need that curled beneath her skin and roared to full life within her belly. Her over-sensitized skin quivered with the play of sensations caressing it. The cool, damp air, the heat of his body against hers, the flex of muscles against her body, and the painful rasp of her constrictive jumpsuit against her skin. Fuck, she hated it. The scientists thought it would serve their needs the best in this environment but she hated the feel of it against her skin, especially now with her senses flooded with more and more tactile information. And now it was a barrier against everything she needed to feel more of as an inferno of need barreled through her.

Whimpering, she clawed uselessly at her clothes until he helped her peel them off. His claws lightly grazed her skin sending a shiver through her, the webbing of his fingers teasing her nipples as they brushed over her breasts, his rough hands sending a delicious sensation through her. When did he remove his gloves? Never mind, it felt too good. She groaned with relief as the jumpsuit dragged free from her legs and she was vaguely aware of it being thrown dismissively into the tree above them after he gave the fabric a disgusted look.

Gwen muffled a laugh, highly entertained by his sentiment. Gods, he was right though. The fabric was terrible. Now that it was finally off of her, she felt like she could finally breathe! The entire world came to life around her.

Gods, is that what the world really felt like? For the first time since she had awakened on Xal, she hadn't stripped her skin and rather than having a sensation of her senses being muted with a haze of pain and the medications within the cream, she felt… everything! She felt so alive. Her arms and legs wrapped around the male covering her, rejoicing in the sensation of his bare body against hers. She didn't know how he removed his clothes so quickly, but she was grateful. Finally, she could get the relief she needed and get it out of her system. She didn't want a mate, didn't want to be bred by anyone—but she needed this. Just this once and then she would be fine and work out what to do with her new life with a clear head.

Zyr's naked body pressed against hers ravenously, matching her hunger for hunger, the ripple of his muscles and textured skin sending pleasure through her skin. She blinked at his chest, watching his markings pick up a glow that they hadn't seemed to possess in the daylight before. She ran her fingers over a spray of them and he groaned, his hand rising to cover hers, keeping it pressed over his heart. Make that hearts. She could feel the double beat of two hearts pounding beneath her palm. His hand and forearm were veined with strength, his claws so similar to hers but longer and more vicious looking than anything than anything either she or Chris had.

Fuck, she still didn't know whether or not he was the one who killed Chris. Was she really going to do this without knowing?

He mouthed her skin as he slid over her, banishing every worry with an intense wave of pleasure. Carefully, he rearranged her limbs, pulling them from around him and turning her so that she faced the tree and was braced against it, giving him her back. She shivered with hyper-awareness, unable to see him and yet that seemed to increase her pleasure as she felt the heat of him and his every touch. It burned through her, every caress of his mouth and the trail of his fingers and claws mapping out the constellations of textures over her skin. Hers didn't glow with colorful splashes like his did, being far less remarkable in her opinion with a splash of teal over her brilliant shade of green, but his every touch lingered upon them as if they were the greatest beauty before dipping lower to stroke the back of her knees.

She moaned, her claws digging into the tree bark in front of her. Why didn't anyone ever tell her that the back of the knee was an erogenous zone?

He crooned to her, his hands gliding along her thighs and up her flanks as he fitted his pelvis against her ass, his chest and belly extending over her back. She did not feel his cock, just the hard bulge of flesh that she had felt before as if his sex was protected beneath a rigid pouch. Even still, it was clearly sensitive since he groaned in her ear with every brush of it against the exposed folds of her sex as his tongue simultaneously stroked along the shell of her very human ear.

"So many beautiful differences," he rasped, his nose nuzzling her pulse beneath her ear.

Warm hands stroked up her belly to cup her breasts, the stretch of webbing that silkily grazed her belly in contrast to the roughness of his hands. It teased her nipples and he trilled with what seemed like fascination as he ran the webbing back and forth over her nipples before teasing them lightly with his claws, making them lengthen and stiffen. She shivered against him, her belly spasming painfully, her channel achingly empty.

"Please, it hurts. I need you."

He murmured soothingly in her ear, one of his hands dipping back down her belly to caress between her legs. She canted into his touch, her breath leaving her on a gasp. Yes, she needed that. Exactly that. His fingers carefully parted her folds and stroked the side of his finger along her weeping slickness so that his claw didn't catch her. Her belly quivered with another rush of arousal, her sex getting impossibly wetter that the glide of his finger squelched softly along the side of her clit, moving faster as she rocketed up to her first orgasm. She detonated and his knuckles pinched her clit sharply, extending the sensation until she shook from the pleasure rolling through her.

She was still trembling with the aftershocks of release when his arms tightened around her and something warm and firm, yet shockingly flexible, pressed into her. It twisted and flicked within her as he rocked his hips, the tip of it stroking like a tongue along the walls of her channel and lapping firmly at her cervix and every sensitive spot around it. Her pussy clenched around his cock as he bottomed out, the hard bulge around the base of his sex brushing her clit as a hard node above it pressed against the bud of her ass.

Gods, it was so good. She rocked her hips against him, her breathing panting out of her as he alternately growled and trilled softly in her ear. His thrusts became more eager, harder in response, his claws pricking hard against her skin in his excitement. Thanks to her skin grafts, it sent pleasure through her, rather than cutting her as they might have if she still possessed the flesh she was born with. At that moment, she was grateful for it and the heightened sensation her new form brought her as their fucking quickly shifted to a ravenous rut, their bodies rocking wildly against each other, their mingling cries lifting through the forest.

She lost count of how many times she spasmed around him, her orgasms drawing her pleasure up higher rather than cooling it. She needed something more and it was maddening. Her claws dug deeper into the wood. She would have used them against him if she had the opportunity as great as her frustration was growing. She snarled and he trilled softly in her ear with a soft chuckle.

"I know," he rasped breathlessly. "Take your frustration out on the tree. There is a reason we turn our females when they are needing, though your claws, as small as they are, might feel pleasurable."

"Why not find out," she gasped, bark breaking free as her claws slipped slightly on their purchase.

"Hmm, perhaps another time," he groaned, his hips snapping furiously as his pace suddenly increased.

His thrusts were coming faster, his breath harsher in her ears as her pleasure rose again at the driving writhing sensations stroking through her. Suddenly he drove deep, the tip of his cock pressing firmly against the entrance of her womb and held as his release flooded her. It wasn't ejaculation like a human but thicker and far more of it as it struck her depths repeatedly with every pulse of his now rigid sex buried in her. The pressure built within her, rising from the depths of her belly like a tsunami or lightning rising from the ground with the way ripped through her. She spasmed hard around him, triggering a harder orgasm from him as he released more of his seed into her. They cried out together, sending wildlife scattering with squawks and shrieks as they rode out their pleasure.

When it finally faded, he slipped off her and gently unhooked her claws from the tree before pulling her into his arms as he dragged her onto his lap. She curled up against him, his hearts thumping at a gradually calming beat beneath her ear as his warmth surrounded her. The morning air was still cool, so his warmth was welcome, and she snuggled into his embrace. This was nice. It was okay for it to be nice.

CHAPTER 5

CHAPTER 5

Zyr held the female in his arms, gazing down at her. She was perfect, everything he could possibly want for a mate. He wasn't sure at first when he caught his initial glimpse of her. She was fleshier than the females of his species and had strange growths from her head that slightly resembled his awgree crest, though typically females had much shorter crests. Her breasts puzzled him too since his species didn't swell there unless they were nursing. As he had observed the strangers with his sister, he had been certain that they were a mated pair with offspring in their odd, metal abode.

He had been disgusted, too. Not due to the female. Although she had been strange to him, it had nothing to do with that. He had been disgusted with himself. He had forgotten his duty to watch over his sister and had left her to follow the enticing vibrations through the water of a female going into heat. It had been what he assumed anyway, until he found the strange golden sphere. He had carried it up into the trees, staring down at it with

35

a mixture of disdain and wonder. Curious at what it was but at the same time annoyed that it had fooled him. He had been so hopeful. Never had he felt so pulled before.

And then his sister arrived and had a good laugh at his expense. They had speculated it to be a Gwyr invention since that species was always devising new technologies that baffled his kind. That was until he saw the strangers return.

He and Eyra were there hidden among the trees when they caught sight of the pair returning to the shelter and watched them for a while in fascination. He could admit to himself now that he had been captivated by the odd female who was clearly similar but different than his species. He knew of no clan who had such appearance or such brilliant colors. The male was a brilliant yellow with black markings, but the female was the color of new leaves during the season of rains.

And now she was his. His rain goddess. He had been partially truthful when he explained that jymlina was the name of a flower—a particularly sweet one that bloomed only during the season of rains—but, more importantly, it was the name of the rain goddess from whom the flower was named. He had called her such privately to himself when he caught sight of the late day sun hitting her flesh and he had felt such disappointment that she was mated already to the yellow one. With his coloring, though, it seemed that they fit even if his gut soured at it.

It was his feelings toward what he perceived as an already mated female that had him quickly departing, dragging his sister away before the strangers spotted him. He just hadn't counted on the younger female's fascination with the yellow male. She got away from Zyr early the next morning, tracking back to the metal shelter to spy upon and follow the object of her fascination. In retrospect, though Zyr had been furious, he hadn't blamed her and ultimately he was grateful—though quite shocked—when the male's painfully terrible song drew forth his sister's needing and triggering the male's rut.

The moment he caught sight of them stripping each other in a tree, their mating scent filling the air, Zyr had rushed away with embarrassment. He hadn't gotten far when he decided to circle around with excitement back to the female who had drawn his attention. Though the mating vibrations had not been hers—and now he doubted that she even possessed them and without the peculiar sphere he probably would never have been aware of her presence—he hadn't been able to resist singing for her. He hadn't been worried about the other male returning and catching him. Since Eyra mated with the yellow one, he knew that she would be returning home with her mate.

And he had gained his own mate.

Zyr nuzzled his female's strange, silky crest that was so much softer than his own stiffer tendrils that were woven down his back, and gently nipped her oddly small, round ears. Everything about her was fascinating and now even more alluring to him. A sense of wellbeing settled over him as he knew that it would once he mated, his desires shifting to please his mate. He still had his duties as prince, but his life would shift significantly now to caring for his mate and any offspring they had and protecting the heart of the clan, leaving the duties of traversing their territory to younger, unmated males.

He never thought he would see the day after so many seasons of failing to find a mate. Female offspring were fewer, their kind breeding more warriors than life-bearers which had been explained to him as a way their kind had evolved to maintain a breeding population. That their biological evolution never caught up to their social evolution sadly meant that they had a surplus of unmated males with their population possessing three males to every female. It wasn't such a sad state as the Gwyr who suffered even fewer females, but it still made breeding competition fierce.

Truly, it was a shame he hadn't thrown the orb further. He had known it would draw other males eager to claim an unmated female, but he couldn't risk leaving her alone for another male to court while he disposed of the contraption. So he hefted it with all his strength and sang, hoping that he would have time before another male would come.

He nuzzled his mate again, pleased. They had come but it had been his victory. He had inspired her heat, his rut falling on him. And though he suffered through it as she ignored his calls and had been forced to discourage the males who hoped to take advantage of an unfulfilled heat to claim a mate, it had all been worth it.

He brushed his nose against her jaw and a tiny puff of air escaped her lips as she sighed in reaction. He smiled to himself and hugged her closer. His. His mate. His smile faded into a frustrated grimace. A mate he didn't even have the name of. He had been so caught up in the scent of her heat with its outpouring of pheromones that he had been too distracted to remember to ask her for her name when he gave his.

She stretched against him, signaling her rousing and he bent over her eagerly to peer down into her face. He couldn't wait for her to awaken and take her home. Sure, he had agreed for them to satisfy her heat with no commitments with the understanding that her kind were not like his, but surely, she would see sense now. After all, they bred. Although there were no guarantees, especially since they weren't the same species, it was possible that they created life. The probability of it seemed promising given that they triggered each other's respective heat and rut. Beyond his fear that she would try to escape him and go through a dangerous time by herself scared him.

How would he convince her to stay if she hadn't come to see reason?

The strange fringe on her eyes flickered and her eyes opened, their water-colored depths of the like that he'd never seen before, peering up at him. She startled briefly but as the haze of sleep cleared from her eyes, she blinked up at him in recognition. She yawned and gently pushed against his chest, signaling that she wanted to sit up. Although he was loath to let her go, he loosened his grip and she sat up in his lap as she rubbed her eyes.

"How are you feeling?" he murmured, his hand stroking over her soft crest.

She cocked her head in consideration and smiled. "Much better. Actually… very relaxed," she added with a laugh.

He bit back a sound of frustration when she slipped off his lap instead of reclining affectionately back into his embrace and stood. Taking his cue from her, he stood as well, stretching the long flexible muscles coiled in his calves and thighs. She gave his legs a startled look as they stretched and lengthened, her shocked gaze traveling to his genital pouch. He grinned over at her even as a deeper worry settled within him of just how vulnerable she would be without the protection of the clan—without him.

"I suppose this is another difference in our species."

"Yeah," she agreed with a small laugh. "My muscles definitely don't do that, and I don't think my skin on my legs is even stretchy enough to allow it. But that is incredible. You must be able to jump like a frog."

He had no idea what a frog was, but pride filled him in response to her admiration. He had longer legs and a greater jump and speed than most males of his clan which made him a formidable warrior and protector. His coloring wasn't particularly distinguished—and certainly not like the male Eyra mated who now would hold that position—but he prided himself that his bioluminescent natri were brighter and more numerous than many could brag of. He didn't point any of that out. She would note what a fine mate she had once she saw the other males of his clan.

Pulling on his trousers and hooking the ends over his feet, he straightened to his full height beside her and held out his hand.

"We should go."

She stared at his offered hand and lifted her puzzled gaze to his face. "Go where?"

"Home. To the clan," he added so that there would be no confusion.

His hope that she would have seen reason with their breeding shattered when she recoiled, and his jaw tightened though he pushed back his disappointment. Her reaction had always been a possibility, so he was not entirely surprised. It seemed that he would have to do more convincing than he thought.

CHAPTER 6

*G*o home. With *him*? She was insane that she was more than a little tempted. She had never felt so safe than she had in his arms or so connected to another person. It was crazy. She wasn't the type to be dick-matized. Good sex, even incredible sex, had never been enough to make her want to make such an impromptu decision. Whatever the scientists had done to her paired with her strange reaction to the alien in front of her was making her behave illogically. It was like she had a whole new set of instincts and desires that she was never born with.

How strange was it that she wanted this future he offered? She shivered as a loud, rattling shriek broke out somewhere deep in the swamp. Okay, and there was that.

What the fuck is that?

Whatever that was it sounded big and vicious, unlike any life-form she and Chris had come across in the swamp. Facing all of that alone was a lot more frightening than her initial decision that had been fueled just by her desire to escape Darvel Corp's plans for her.

Now she felt like she was facing her future, and he was wearing a disappointed look on his face. It pained her to know that it was because of her. She had pushed him away, but she had to think. This male had possibly been the one to kill Chris, and while that might be considered the law of nature among his species for all she knew, that still didn't set right with her human sensibilities.

There was also the matter of him mentioning his clan that made her nervous. It wasn't that she objected to safety. She was a *big* fan of safety. But the idea of being surrounded by a whole lot of aliens who could see her presence as a threat made her very nervous.

"Wait. Slow down. You want me to go home... with you... to live among your clan?" she asked nervously.

His head tilted and he peered back at her as he caught her hand in his. "There is no reason to be frightened. We will live in the heart of our lands in the primary clan pod. There are small pods of our relations scattered throughout our waters, of course, but you will have plenty of kin surrounding you."

Great, so it was worse than she thought. Not only would she be surrounded by strange aliens, but she would likely not even be able to escape them. If they ganged up on her... no, she couldn't do it. As much as a significant part of her craved to be near him, she couldn't go with him. She would go mad.

Slowly she pulled her hand free and shook her head, taking a cautious step away from him on the enormous tree limb beneath their feet. Although it was wider than most walkways, she wasn't so foolish not to be at least a little careful of her movements.

"I'm sorry, but I don't think that is a good idea."

He hissed softly but the sound of it was not aggressive. She could hear the note of exasperation as he stared at her.

"I am trying to be understanding of our differences, but this resistance to what is natural is ridiculous. You must know that among my people we are a mated pair. All of my kin will know I am mated the moment they see me. My pheromones have changed, and they will scent it. All will wonder where my mate is."

She frowned and leaned forward, sniffing in his direction. "I don't smell anything."

He hissed again with vexation. "Your species' sense of smell is under-developed then. I can smell it as clearly as I can scent yours, though admittedly your pheromone trail is not as strong as a Bai."

"Bai is your species?" At his nod, she gave another sniff before giving up with an apologetic shrug. "Yeah, human noses just don't do it, I guess. You smell nice but not any different than before."

Nice was an understatement. There was something very appealing to it, like lotus and amber with a dark undertone. She could drink in his scent all day and never get tired of it. She wished that she were in his arms again so that she could be surrounded with it and his wonderful warmth. Biting back of groan, she pushed that particular desire to the back of her mind. That line of thinking wasn't going to help her out any.

"Whether you can perceive it as we can, the change is there. Mating is sacred and the most important achievement of an adult male's lifespan. And within that of our females as well. It is not something that we discard. Our mates are of the highest importance and not one of us would agree to such separation. Solidifying our nest is the next natural step. How is it that the male with you understood this, but you do not?"

"What? What about Chris?" She stared at him in shock. Was it possible that Chris was still alive? The madness gripping her made her want to forget her questions and embrace what the alien offered but this… this was important.

"Chris," he agreed, the name heavily accented on his tongue.

She felt almost weak with the relief that suddenly hit her. "I thought you killed him."

Now Zyr was the one who looked surprised. "Kill him? For what reason? True, I was envious of him at first when I thought he was your mate, but we don't kill for mating rights. Competition can get fierce but never that bad. Only in the most extreme and depraved cases has that happened within the history of the Bia clans. We are not Gwyr."

"Memo me, don't be claimed by a Gwyr," she muttered.

Zyr puffed up and glowered possessively. "You will not be going anywhere near the Gwyr. They are a mountain-dwelling species filled with depravity. I will not have you anywhere near them and their experiments. You are *my* mate."

"Relax, I have no intention of doing so," she snorted. "Now, continue with what you were saying about Chris. Is he okay?"

"He sang... terribly," he chuckled, "but it drew my younger sister to him who was under my guard. Now she is his responsibility, and mine no more. It was only by chance that I was drawn to your orb, and although because of that my sister found her mate, I did not believe I would share the same fortune. Never have I been happier to be wrong."

"I just don't understand why this matters so much. Human relationships are not like this," she protested. "We just find someone we like and see if there is enough chemistry and commonalities for us to remain together. It isn't some huge imperative like you make it out to be. You act like I'm the culmination of everything you have wanted, and you just met me."

"Because you are." A sweet smile pulled at his lips, though it showed the dangerous sharp points of his teeth, and she felt a warmth settle in her chest at his earnest words. "As a prince, I have done my duty and sung for hundreds of females amid these waters and those of distant territories and never drew a mate. Before you came, I was cursed to live a half-life as an outcast amid the waters, until now."

"Cursed? That is a bit extreme," she replied with an uneasy laugh, but it died at the solemn expression on his face.

"How so?" He gave her an inquisitive look. "A male without a mate is a male with little worth. He can hunt and provide for those who need extra assistance from time to time so long as the mated male of the family permits it, but he does not yield new generations. His line is doomed to die with little comfort. And while there are those who earn their way by hunting or engaging in various tasks as much as they can, for a prince it is seen as a disfavor of the gods. For many turns of the seasons, I have been shunned but now it has ended. I will take good care of you, jymlina. You will not want for anything. You will be safe from the dangers of this world."

She swallowed and looked away. She hated the contractual aspect. She didn't want him to think that she would just be with him for the sake of safety. "I'm doing all right."

"You are," he agreed slowly as he approached nearer. He reached out, his hand stroking soothingly down her arm. "For now. But you have left the protection of your shelter."

"It wasn't safe there any longer. No place near there is safe, not when they come to retrieve it."

"When who comes?" He buffed his knuckles against her cheek.

She leaned into the touch instinctively. How was it that his skin did not feel wrong? The texture of his slid against her flesh, exciting her. She forcibly pulled away from it to look him in the eye. He had to be aware of the danger.

"Those who sent me. They will look for me and then they will destroy all evidence that I was ever here. I can't stay here, and you need to warn your people so that no one goes near that place." She hesitated with uncertainty. Regardless of what she ended up deciding, she couldn't leave it there and take the chance of someone getting hurt. "If you bring the orb, I can deactivate it so that it does not draw anyone else."

"I do not wish to leave your side," he muttered unhappily.

"I'll be fine," she assured him. "I was safe here all night. You don't need to worry."

"Yes, you were safe," he reluctantly admitted. "But I was here watching over you the entire time. I will worry if I leave you here. You have not been hunted by the great graniikal that hides in the darkest parts of the waters, or worse. The thwarik that makes its nests among the trees and drops from the skies and easily pluck up unsuspecting prey who are not quick enough to evade it. These are not the only dangerous, simply among the most terrible. You have been here but for a short time and do not know how to hide from them or evade them."

A shiver of unease ran up her spine. There were really that many predators? She didn't want to sound like a complete wimp by doing a one-eighty quickly but suddenly she very much didn't want to be sitting out there alone in a tree given what she had heard just a few minutes ago. If it was that big and that deadly—and she decidedly wasn't speedy—it was stupid to stay out there.

"I suppose I could just go with you, though I know that I'll just slow you down."

A grin stretched across his face and extended his hand for hers again. "This is an excellent idea, and you do not need to worry about being slow. I will carry you."

"I don't see how that would be a solution," she remarked skeptically. "Carrying me isn't going to help you run quickly either."

He chuckled and his eyes gleamed luminously. It was all the warning she got before he made his move, catching her up in his arms before she even realized what he intended. She barely had time to loop her arms around his neck before he crouched, his muscles tightening, and leapt. She didn't mean to scream, and certainly not in his ear, but finding herself suddenly airborne as if she had just been fired by the ass from a slingshot, she couldn't help herself. She would apologize later when her heart was no longer trying to claw its way up her throat.

With every landing of his feet upon a tree branch they were off again, being propelled through the air as he gradually made his way lower approaching the water surface. Gwen's claws sank into the back of his neck as she watched the water speed toward them.

"Wait, what are we doing?" she cried out.

She could breathe underwater thanks to her modifications but the idea of being encased in that dark gloom of the swamp water made her heart race with terror.

"Water is safety," he shouted. "We swim from here. Hold on!" And with that he plunged them into the cool surface, the water breaking all around them as it swallowed her screams.

CHAPTER 7

The cool shelter of the water surrounded them bringing a familiar peace with it away from the noise and immediate dangers of the surface world. Zyr embraced it, his hearts feeling full as he carried his mate deeper. Though there were predators that hunted through the water, they were far easier to detect and avoid when one could feel the disturbances from their passage. It was rare for any of them to be taken completely unaware, though caution still needed to be taken when it came to the cunning creatures. It was for that reason that he continued to carry his female. That, and the sheer pleasure he had just swimming with her held against his body and within his arms.

He cursed inwardly. He still had not gotten her name from her. He would need to do so before he had any witnesses. He would be teased for ages if they had an audience and it became common knowledge. What sort of male mounts without getting the name of his mate first at the very least? In all fairness, he had been considerably overwhelmed from days of being tormented by the scent of her need but, all the same, he had acted thoughtlessly without observing proper respect and tending toward his female.

He would get it when they stopped, after she disabled the orb that threatened to bring danger to his clan. It still unnerved him to realize that something that was so small and seemed to be little more than a terrible inconvenience could actually lead to death of any one of his people if caught unaware.

They swam for some distance in the quiet beauty of the water, the world around them cast in a glow of golds and greens with a shimmer of blue above, closer to the surface. He glanced down at his mate. He could not understand why she had screamed or had been so hesitant about dropping into this world that offered them so much safety. It was incomprehensible.

He kicked his legs, pushing them through the water swiftly as the thick webbing on his feet caught the water easily to propel him. He had not bothered to strip off his gloves, but it did not matter. His hands were not free anyway since he had his mate in his arms and he would not risk her swimming on her own… not outside of the central breeding grounds of the pod anyway. Since the structure of her legs were so clearly different than his own despite the similar webbing between their digits, there was no way she could swim as fast. She would not only not be able to keep up with him but would be a target for any of the predators that normally left the Bia alone.

Now where is the sphere? It should be around here somewhere.

Diving deeper where the water was darkest, he scanned the muddy bottom, pushing aside the long grasses that he swam between and thin reeds that obscured his view. Shafts of sunlight pierced the water more in some places than in others and he smiled as a beam of light a short distance away caught along a glossy surface with a golden shimmer.

There!

Tightening his arms around his female, he kicked forward hard, enjoying the small bite of her claws into his hide. He dropped his head briefly to give her a fond look before refocusing again on his target as they rapidly made their approach. Angling his body, he dropped down lower. His mate turned slightly in his grip to peer over her shoulder and he knew the moment she spotted the object by the excited jump of her muscles beneath his hands. Releasing one hand from around him, she pointed to it and grinned up at him. He nodded, returning her smile, and dropped the final span of distance. His right arm slipped from her warm softness as he prepared to reach out for the object. He was now close enough that its hum overpowered his preoccupation with his mate to notice it but rather than excite him it sent an unpleasant current over his skin.

Logically, he knew that was due to his chemical change in response to mating that would prevent him from attempting to seek out another mate, but it was still disconcerting. Though the sphere was definitely not a potential mate-seeking female, that knowledge did not do anything to relieve him of his instinctual response to it. Pushing back his unsettled feeling as he neared it, Zyr stretched out his hand and scooped it up from the mud. The debris sifted off of it the moment it was disturbed from its resting place, causing it to glow brighter as he handed it to his female. He was far more comfortable with her handling it and she was happily very obliging as she relieved him of it without hesitation.

Zyr shifted his grip on her, tightening his hold since his mate was no longer able to cling to him as she had been with her hands now otherwise occupied, and rose back up to a more comfortable depth as he began to speed forward once more. Below them grasses off different hues and shades passed, some of them brilliant enough to catch the attention of the female in his arms so that she openly gawked at them, much to his amusement.

Finally, they surfaced a safe distance from the metal abode. Just in case the humans returned sooner than his mate feared. He was taking no chances. Allowing just his head to break the surface of the water, he held his mate tucked in close to his chest, still submerged and glanced around, his nostrils flaring to take in the scents as his eyes focused on points far from him in search of any sign of danger. Satisfied that they were safe enough, he plunged beneath the water again to swim over to the nearest root system of one of the great trees and pushed his mate up upon it before climbing out after her.

She blinked back the water streaming down her face as she brushed back her wet crest that clung to every part of her it touched. His own, arranged to fall down his back, sloughed water easily rather than drip continuously as hers did and for a moment he felt a sense of pity for the annoyance she surely had to suffer because of it. She did not seem to notice though. She merely brushed it back and mopped her face with one hand, her entire attention focused on the orb in her hand. Crouching beside where she sits on the thick, twisted root beneath her, he watched curiously as her fingers tap at various points of the part of the sphere facing upward at her. Each point glows and gibbers in an unfamiliar language. She replies back to it, the strange words falling off her tongue quickly as she continues to work it—finally the sphere's glow fades, leaving nothing but its solid casing as if the life went out of it.

"Finished?" Zyr glanced at her curiously.

"All done," she replied, handing the cold metal back to him.

He could take it back with them and give it to their scientists and scholars to look at it, but his skin shuddered at the idea of it accidentally being turned on. Without a qualm, he drew his arm back and bashed it against the hard root of the tree, making his female jump with surprise, until it cracked like a nut in his hand. He then tossed it back out into the water, watching with satisfaction as it sank from sight.

"Well, that's one way to do it," she observed with a laugh. Her gazed lingered for a moment on his arms. "You are definitely very strong. I didn't even think that was possible."

He preened at her praise and crept closer to her, his fingers brushing through her soaked crest, pushing it back over her shoulders. "Strength is good, but it is best when you have a family—a mate—to protect with it. What strength I possess is yours whenever you might require or have need of it."

Her brows raised a bit as if not entirely able to believe his declaration, but she smiled and leaned into his touch.

"I suppose I can't object to that," she murmured, humor lacing her words and he grinned in response to her sudden spark of playfulness.

Bia, as a species, enjoyed play considerably and seeing his female's mood lightening in such a way pleased him greatly. It was not by much, but it was a start and that gave him hope.

She sighed and gave him a thoughtful look. "I suppose that means now we go… to your clan." She grimaced and he regarded her with confusion.

What was all her objection about returning to his clan? He did not understand. Clan breeding grounds were fortified and safe. Why would she dread it?

Gently, he squeezed her arm until her water-colored eyes turned back up on him. "Why do you dislike returning to my clan? There are comforts there and protection that could not be had in the wilds of our world." He paused, a terrible thought occurring to him, wounding his hearts. "Or is it that you hate being mated to me so much that you do not wish for the others to know? They would know anyway by scent but if you are ashamed to be my mate…" His voice trailed off.

It seemed so improbable. He was an agreeable male. He had made a mistake in his eagerness with his mate, but he had stepped outside of convention to agree to her terms—and would have left her as they agreed had she insisted to leave him even if it broke his heart—so that she would be comfortable. He did not think he was unattractive and as a prince he had the power to give her more than some.

She stared at him, her mouth falling open.

"What? No! Of course, that's not it. I mean this is really, *really*, fast for me but I'm kind of seeing the benefits of it and actually, as strange as it seems, do want to stay with you. The idea of being away from you makes me feel ill. It's not you. You are wonderful and have been very patient and kind with all of this." She glanced down at her hands where her claws are plucking at the webbing.

He reached over and stilled her fingers with his hand, a concerned frown pulling on his mouth. "Do not damage your webbing. It can be surgically repaired but it will never be truly the same afterward and will still give you pain."

She glanced at her claws in surprise and immediately flattened her hands against her thighs. Drawing in a deep breath, she spoke again, uncertainty laden in her voice.

"Look, I get that this is natural for you and how you feel about this… ah… mating, but your clan may not feel the same way about it."

Understanding dawned and his hearts melted with sympathy. "You worry that they will react poorly to you?" She gave a small nod, and he caressed her arms, sliding his hands up to her shoulders. "You do not need to have such worries," he murmured. "You may not be Bia, but you share many similarities with us. But more importantly, it is understood that this thing is not something that can be chosen. It is instinct. My clan will celebrate."

An unhappy look crossed her face and he stilled, uncertain of what he said wrong.

"Right. Instinct," she muttered and a soft sigh puffed from her lips.

Zyr slowly dragged her to his chest, his hand shifting to stroke her back. "It is a good foundation. We will be happy because I will make sure that I will do all that I can to make sure that you are."

Another puff of air escaped her, this time with a hint of amusement as she looked up at him. "You do know that you are not responsible for my happiness, right?"

He prickled in offense but calmed. She did not understand his culture. "Of course, it is. Mates working to assure each other's happiness and that of their young and their kin is part of what makes Bia society strong. It is why my clan will accept you, because they care for me and you are everything for me now. Already I know that you will become the joy of my heart. I am already well on my way to that state," he admitted, brushing his nose over the top of her head.

She peered up at him, a look of understanding flooding her features. "I think I understand a little."

"Good." He hugged her to him, enjoying the press of her smaller body against his.

Her nose nuzzled his chest, her breath warm on his skin. "So, I suppose it's time for us to go?"

He was about to nod but paused. "First, before I take you to meet the clan… there is something I must know."

She tipped her head back, her brow furrowing. "What is that?"

Zyr cleared his throat uncomfortably. "What is your name?"

He prepared for a sound or look of offense. Her brows winged up and a look of surprise crossed her face. And then… she laughed. The laughter was loud and bold, and possessed a peel of merriment to it that lightened his soul. And it was the most beautiful sound he ever heard.

"Gwen. It's Gwen," she said.

Correction. Her laughter was the second most beautiful thing, for her name was surely the most beautiful sounds ever put together.

CHAPTER 8

*T*heir arrival within the central pod breeding grounds was met with curious looks. With the late hour and the fall of darkness, the activity of the pod had slowed but there were many vendors still out with their wares. The cooler hours allowed them to conduct business comfortably for the small spurts of Bia who traveled from their homes to acquire supplies that they needed. It was these members of his pod whose eyes followed them. There was no maliciousness in their gazes to agitate Zyr so he smiled politely and led his mate among them, her hand entwined with his.

Although Gwen had reached for his hand the moment he had set her on her feet outside the borders of the breeding ground, called that for the closely guarded territory where they lived and raised their young, he had been very pleased by the small gesture. Bia were a very tactile and affectionate species. Public embraces and shows of affection, even as simple as holding hands so that the sensitive webbing of their fingers could brush were not only enjoyed but seen in a favorable light by the rest of the clan. By entering with their hands clasped it sent a very clear message to those who saw them of their already forming bond and nothing could make him happier. He caught more than one smile as they passed, and his chest puffed out with joy.

He understood Gwen's fears and probably would have had similar feelings of uncertainty if it were he going to dwell among her people without any knowledge of what to expect, but he hoped that she was seeing all of this. She was certainly busying herself trying to look everywhere at once, to his amusement. Surely, she saw that there was not one suspicious look, just open curiosity and interest, and happiness in the eyes of those who knew him the best and knew how long he had waited for this moment. If there were any at all who felt otherwise, they wisely kept it to themselves and went about their business. As he had told his mate, this was simply the way of their species. A new mating was never cursed or unwanted by the clan. It brought them strength as a people.

Finally, they arrived at the white palace. The pale stone with its threads of green and gold mineral deposits was a royal family complex at the very heart of the central pod. It alone stood out among the green stone buildings that made up their family dwellings and places of business so that it was always easy to find for any member of the clan regardless of what pod they came from. Warriors stationed at the gate inclined their heads in acknowledgement as he passed.

Since he had spent much of his time since reaching adulthood and failing to find a mate out patrolling the waters of their clan territory, it had been many revolutions since he had returned to the white palace. Zyr was grateful to see that little changed. He pulled his mate after him as he headed toward the throne room, aware of the sound of Gwen's footwear sloshing behind him. He did not understand how she could wear her human clothing. The footwear in particular struck him as particularly uncomfortable and confining. Did it simply trap the water around the foot? He shuddered and nearly offered to take them to their rooms where he could see about finding her something more suitable to wear.

As expected, when they entered the throne room, it was empty but not for long. Word always traveled quick around the palace and within a short amount of time his mother hustled in, her once vivid, dark blue coloring faded to a pale gray blue with her age. Her eyes widened at the sight of them, a smile breaking out over her face as her eyes crinkled happily.

"Zyr! You have returned... and with a mate!" She bestowed a curious glance toward Gwen, and he grinned, eager to make the introductions.

"Mother, this Gwen. She is not Bia but has become one of us by the will of the gods." He turned toward his mate, drawing her forward in front of him. "Jymlina, this is my mother, Queen Azana."

His mother's eyes brightened with interest. "Another like Eyra's mate, and just as brightly colored. How fascinating! Eyra did say that there was a female like her Chris. It makes me wonder how many more like them are within our lands."

"We are the only ones," Gwen replied. "Our species does not normally look like this but we were changed to be adaptable to this planet and sent down here." She made a face. "We were meant to be a mated pair, I guess you would call it, as we made our observations about this planet for possible human habitation. Our species in our original form possess soft skin, and no claws or webbing, among other minor changes. We cannot breathe water in our original form."

His mother's brow raised with interest. "It hardly seems likely that this world would be a kind one for those who have not undergone the changes that you have. But what is your prognosis? Are more of your species coming here?"

"I do not know," Gwen admitted. "It is complicated since there is clearly intelligent alien life here and there has already been trouble before over Corp trying to colonize on such worlds and trying to cover it up. If they try again, it likely won't be here so that there aren't inquiries made. But they most certainly will be destroying evidence that Chris and I were here. They may try to send a team to another continent to see if it is uninhabited since that is legally permissible to a degree but I'm not sure if they will or not."

His mother's mouth pinched, but then she sighed. "It is a good thing, then, that they are not coming here if they will bring trouble with them. Bia live peacefully within our territories with only the occasional disputes. Too much of our daily lives is about protecting ourselves from the multitude of dangers that exist in our world. If you and Chris were adapted to live here, I would be afraid for a species who lacked such adaptions." She paused meaningfully. "For, not of. We are perfectly capable of defending ourselves, but we would not need to destroy an invading species, the swamp would do it for us, I believe. I am not convinced that your kind would be able to survive here."

"There is another thing, mother," Zyr interrupted, and he quickly explained the situation that happened with the golden sphere.

She nodded, a worried look crossing her face. "And it distinctly felt like those of a female?"

He nodded. "Specifically, one receptive of mating."

His mother cursed softly and cast a worried look to his older sister, the next in line for the throne. "We will send out an alert to the other pods and territories to be aware of such signals and approach with caution."

"It is possible that Darvel Corp will change the signal. It was an observation that I reported that your appearance coincided with the activation of the sphere."

"Noted," his mother replied gravely. She sighed and gave them both a fond look. "But now is not a time of worry. You have dealt with the immediate threat and we will alert our people to stay away from that part of territory until the humans have disposed of their 'evidence.' Now we will celebrate this happy occasion. My son, my third born, has finally mated and returned home. There will be feasts arranged for the entire clan to celebrate all throughout our territory. For now, however, take your mate to your rooms, Zyr. Settle in and get some well deserved rest."

"Yes mother," he murmured as he bowed his head with a small smile.

"And Gwen, welcome to the family," his mother added as she reached forward and grasped his mate's hand in her own bared hand in a show of familiarity and family.

Giving it a small squeeze, she beamed and left with his sister and her small entourage, leaving Zyr alone with his mate. Gwen glanced at him, her lips curving.

"I can't believe that just happened," she whispered.

He raised his brow in question, and she laughed, her shoulder nudging his as she leaned into him.

"I mean that she was nice and so accepting. The queen! Your mom! And she didn't even care that we aren't the same species— that I'm not just somebody non-gratas dumped on your world."

Now he was confused. "Non-gratas?"

She shook her head, her smile dimming slightly. Whatever it was, it wasn't good, and he was pained that his mate had ever been made to feel less than she was. "I will explain later. But first, show me to our rooms."

With a grin, he grabbed her hand in his once more, enjoying the glide of her webbing against his and drew her with him as he led her through the halls. He understood that the Gwyr had tall buildings that stretched toward the sky unlike the Bia who preferred everything low and concealed. There were no great, towering structures here, not even in the palace, but the sprawl of the palace covered much ground and eventually they found their way into his private wing which was comprised of numerous apartments constructed after his birth to hold not only him and his mate but his children and grandchildren.

He opened the door to his rooms and grinned at the way his mate stared at their surroundings with interest as he pressed the button to ignite the systems that powered the space. The lights slowly brightened, chasing away the gloom to show off the architecture and various art that he had collected as a young male and contraptions he had been fascinated with… a toy that moved independently as it played music and appeared to dance without being hooked to a complex hydro-system that powered the pod. It was one of several Gwyr designs that had somehow made its way down into the territory into the markets of the central pod. He had studied it for many lunar cycles, fascinated with how it worked. Now it couldn't compare to the fascination he felt for the female peering at everything with some sort of fascination that he had felt, everything as new and strange to her that Gwyr toy had been.

Slowly, she made her way over to the large round sleeping hollow built deep into the wall. It was a sizeable hollow, large enough that he could stand on the thick bedding and stretch his hands over his head and just barely graze the roof of it with the tips of his claws and wide enough to easily fit three or four adult Bia laying side by side. Gwen grinned, a spark of pleasure in her eyes when she touched the bedding woven of hagelia fronds that captured the moisture in the air to keep them soft without being abrasively dry against sensitive Bia skin. Apparently, this was another commonality they shared, but then, he knew that her skin was sensitive. He had seen that for himself when he ran his claws over her.

His cock twitched at the memory, and he palmed its hard, protective sheath, swallowing as he watched his mate with hungry eyes. He did not wish to be an impatient or demanding mate, especially not when his female was captivated in her exploration, but his rut was returning with a vengeance. She was still in heat, even if the symptoms had died down, and would be for several days yet, stirring his rut into life with small periods of rest in between. It seemed that their reprieve was over though she had not noticed yet.

She continued to slide her hand over the fabric in wonder and gradually he became aware of her heat increasing. He could feel it from where he stood and the ache in his cock intensified. Her breaths became sharper in tiny pants and a shiver ran over her skin, visible where it was exposed to the air, the smell of her blooming arousal filling his nose. His cock whipped hard within its sheath making his body tremble with lust. Soon it would extrude, pushing its way from the sheath's sensitive slit, the only soft spot on the genital guard. An exquisite pleasure filled him as he felt the pressure of it pushing out, folding back the fleshy area of his sheath. His own pheromone output was increasing but she was so nose blind that she did not notice.

He knew the moment that she became aware of her increasing arousal. Her hand trembled as she turned toward him, her pupils blown out. She shivered, her flesh gleaming with her aroused state.

"Zyr?" she panted, her voice soft and breathy.

He approached slowly, holding himself back the best he could so not to startle her with his greater speed. "It is just your heat. The intensity of your need will come and go for the next few days. A newly mated pair doesn't leave their rooms for several days, not until the heat ends. A male in rut is not the most pleasant," he added wryly and inwardly chuckled at the look of disbelief she shot him.

"That's hard to believe. You have been nothing but sweet."

"I have not been forced to entertain a room full of unmated males either," he reminded her. "They would not try to pursue you, but it will not stop me from feeling possessive and jealous of having you anywhere near them while you are in heat."

"Ah," she murmured, and a mischievous smile pulled at her lips. "So, this heat, it does things to you... this rut you are talking about. Don't take this wrong... but I'm glad I'm not the only one suffering. But at least that is something we can easily do something about."

Gwen walked toward him, her entire body singing with her need as she kicked off her footwear and slowly peeled off her clothing, baring the delightful full swells of her breasts, the softness of her belly, and the sweet lushness of her hips and thighs. Hastily he stripped, aware of his mate's eyes on his sheath, wanting to be naked and ready when she was. As the material dropped to the floor around her feet, her intoxicating smell filled his nose, and a sense of euphoria flooded him as his cock pushed free.

Her eyes widened. "Wow," she whispered. "So that's what I felt." She moved in closer, trailing her fingers over his sheath, and smiled when he shivered. "It's hard."

"To protect my genitals," he murmured and nearly gasped when her hand slicked over his cock.

Beneath her hand the slick flesh widened and flattened and bulged out as its core bulged. She gaped down at it in fascination, her hand working it as it writhed, its shape changing subtly, flattening and thickening alternately until his eyes practically rolled into the back of his head. With a growl he gripped Gwen and attempted to turn her, but she stilled him, a look of heated challenge in her eyes.

"Lay down on the bed."

He stared back at her in disappointment, his hands slipping off her arms. She wished to sleep? He glanced forlornly at the mating pole and looked back at her.

"Don't look at me like that," she whispered. "Just get on the bed. Trust me."

Casting her a doubtful look, he did as she asked and laid flat on the bedding, uncertain of what to expect. He jumped slightly as her soft flesh sliding over him. Whatever he might have guessed at, it definitely wasn't his mate covering him with a shy grin. Sliding over him, she brushed her hot, wet slit against his sheath, rubbing against him as his cock twitched and lashed between them. Her head tossed back as she groaned and slid her hips back and forth, his cock pulsing as the strange fleshy parts of her slit and a rigid bead at its top massaged it. He wanted to grab her hips and hold her in place to ready her for his penetration, but he fisted his hands in the bedding, holding back.

She whispered several intelligible words, but he ignored them, his entire attention fixed on where her hand suddenly grasped his whipping cock once more to press the tip into the heated center of her. His cock immediately stiffened, and he instinctively grabbed ahold of her hips, pressing his own hips up as he thrust deep, his cock twisting subtly in her the entire way until it bottomed out to press and flick against the entrance to her womb. He could not have stopped himself from drawing back to thrust again even if he wanted to. He had little room to move beneath her, but he rocked his hips back and forth. Suddenly she lifted herself up despite his attempt to hold her tightly to him and he let out a frustrated growl.

His claws scraped lightly over her hips, unwilling to hurt her but equally desperate to keep her from leaving him to suffer through his rut. But then she dropped her bottom, driving him deep once more, and he gasped in surprise. He did not recall ever hearing of this. The position was strange to him as it was custom for Bia to mate against a mating pole which had been erected in the corner of his room since he reached maturity but having her move over him sent an overwhelming rush of lust through his veins.

His fingers tightened and he began to move her hips, helping her lift and dragging her down with every drop as he thrust up into her hot sheath. Her channel squeezed around him, rippling as she panted and whimpered, her small claws biting into his skin delivering exquisite stings. It was just as pleasurable as he had imagined. He groaned, increasing his pace as she bounced on him until his frustration peaked. As pleasurable as it was, it was not enough.

With a growl, he flipped them, dropping his female into the bedding beneath him. She cried out as his swollen cock yanked free from her cunt, her fingers digging into the bedding. There was something so perfect about the way she looked up at him with heat in her eyes that he felt suddenly inspired. Rather than flipping her, he held her in place, his hand lightly pressing against her chest as he buried himself between her legs. Her breasts jiggled delightfully with his every thrust. He palmed one, enjoying her response as he rubbed her nipple with his webbing and plucked it between the dull sides of his claws. Her channel spasmed around him, dragging on his cock and he rutted harder, his hips snapping sharply to drive him deeper and faster.

She was his, utterly his, and he couldn't get enough of her.

Every curl of his cock within it, every hard lap where it flattened sent new, fresh jolts of pleasure through him. He moaned, his back arching with the spiral of pleasure rising higher through him. He squeezed her hip with his opposite hand and stroked it before allowing his fingers to stray to the small bud that he noted brought her so much pleasure. He flicked his finger against it and her channel spasmed again with a soft cry from her lips.

He cocked his head, considering it for a moment and then leaned forward, dipping his head down before allowing his tongue to extend to its full length. Equipped with a tongue that was long for foraging fruits and other nutrition from higher reaches, it served him far better than he could dream. Her musky sweetness flooded his mouth, and he growled as his tempo grew wild. Her channel spasmed and then bore down on his cock, dragging hard on it, causing his pleasure to explode through him as white light fired behind his eyes.

Their mutual cries filled the room and beneath his mate glowed so brilliantly green that she appeared as a rare gem but far more glorious. Though she had no bioluminescence that the Bia possessed, she did not need it to glow with her happiness.

Panting, he smiled lovingly down at her. His mate, his heart, his joy and love. Leaning down, he brushed his nose against hers.

"My hearts are yours, for all of my days," he murmured.

A smile lit her face, her hand lifting to caress the side of his jaw. He turned his head to kiss her palm and a happy sigh escaped her.

"I love you, too, Zyr. However this happened, I love you too," she whispered, awe filling her voice as her eyes shined up at him.

With a smile he sank beside her and drew her up into his arms, maneuvering just enough to get the bedding rearranged enough to pull over them. They still had the rest of her heat to ride out—and what pleasure that would be—and a feast to look forward to, but for now they had this moment of peace with a wonderful future stretching out ahead of them. Wherever distant place she came from, it was surely a chance miracle or the favor of the gods that brought her there for him to find.

A smile curled her lips as he nuzzled her jaw. It was a moment to savor and he did.

CHAPTER 9

*G*wen scratched her neck nervously as she stood at Zyr's side. Although the entire clan had been nice to her she kept expecting the other foot to drop. It had taken five days for her heat to pass, and although it had mortified her, it had not seemed to surprise anyone. She had suddenly understood exactly how the queen had been confident at planning a lavish feast with practically no notice. Clearly no one expected them to come up for air any time soon. Food was delivered to their rooms with polite little knocks. Sometimes they enjoyed the food immediately, and other times they ate it a good hour or two later.

It had been extraordinary. Whenever they weren't caught up rutting through her heat, they spent the time talking. Zyr educated her about life among the Bai as much as he could, and she had explained to him her life on United Earth and as a non-gratas. He had been horrified in equal measure to how impressed she was with how Bia society provided a base living for everyone with an opportunity to be and do more beyond that. There was a very tight connection between the members of the clan that she had not been quite able to believe until she saw it. Just like part of her had been entirely certain if her feelings for Zyr would fade once her heat went away. To her surprise, the opposite had been true.

Smiling, she accepted a glass of fermented juice that she didn't quite catch the name of and brought it to her lips as she leaned into her mate's warm body. She hadn't dreamed that at the end of this that she would be so content and happy.

"It's amazing, isn't it?"

She startled and swallowed wrong, nearly choking as she whirled to face the owner of the voice that spoke behind her. Chris grinned at her expression and a lavender female Bai pressed against him regarded Gwen with a look of amusement on her face.

"Chris!" Gwen sighed in relief. She had been hoping to see him but the subject of it just hadn't come up while she was distracted with her heat and attentively loving mate. She suddenly felt a little guilty that she hadn't made more of an effort. That didn't stop her from glowering at him, however. "So glad you weren't eaten by anything," she added drily.

His smile turned sheepish. "Yeah. Sorry about that. I wanted to return but Eyra thought it would be a bad idea."

The female at his side snorted mirthfully. "Chris, you would have stood no chance against my brother. Mated or not, he would have felt threatened while in full rut. You would not have been able to get even a span from the door." She directed a kind smile toward Gwen. "We did make an attempt since Chris was so concerned that he would be worried—it made me a little jealous I admit though I understood. The moment I saw Zyr, however I knew that was it."

"Wise choice," Zyr murmured, his eyes gleaming down at his sister. "This was a strange enough courtship without throwing in another confused human making it more complicated. I might have never gotten her out of the metal structure."

Gwen rolled her eyes. "It was more Corp that sealed that situation up the moment I told them that you were stalking me out there."

Chris's eyebrows flew up in shock. "What?"

She grimaced. "They lost their shit. They planned to have me go into stasis and retrieve me while they destroy any sign that we were here once they found out that there was an alien courtship going on. And more importantly, a sentient alien species."

Chris shook is head and hugged his mate tighter to him. "Well, I have no regrets. This was entirely unexpected but the best thing that's ever happened in my whole life." He gave her a brief smile. "No offense, Gwen, but we didn't exactly click."

"None taken," she replied with a chuckle. "That fact did not escape me."

He gave her a grateful smile. "It was the strangest thing, though, one minute I am outside because I smell the most incredible thing and then these strange sounds start coming from me and that smell gets better and... well," a look of embarrassment flitted across his face. "I'm sure you know what happens after all that."

"All too well," she agreed, giving Zyr a sly smile.

His lips curved in response as they privately shared a memory of that moment. Chris cleared his throat, his eyes shifting between them with amusement.

"So I see. The whole 'we are now mated, and you must come home with me' sort of took me by surprise but it just felt right."

"It was as it should be," Eyra corrected, hugging her mate's arm. Her eyes danced between Gwen and Zyr, and she tugged on Chris's arm. "Come on, Chris, I think they might like a moment of privacy. Congratulations and welcome to the clan, Gwen," she called out as she pulled him away.

Gwen watched them depart, a warmth settling into her chest. Though she had heard that Chris was mated to Zyr's sister she hadn't quite believed that they were as happy as she was. Zyr had said it was just the way Bia society and instinct was, but it had still been a little hard to entirely believe despite living it. Now the knowledge had settled within her, and she wrapped her arms around her mate's side, hugging him to her. His hand stroked down her back, and he looked down at her lovingly as a male who had just arrived talked earnestly to him. Some cousin or another.

Family. Clan. She was one of them and she couldn't wait to see what happened next. And if Darvel Corp was smart, they wouldn't return because the queen was right. Though she and Chris were barely adapted enough to live there, humans were not built to survive on that world. She hoped that they never returned. But if they did it, it was on them. The rest of her life was tied to Zyr and the clan. She owed nothing to the Corp anymore. She was no longer a non-gratas experiment that they could control or own. She belonged to Zyr and his clan, and they belonged to her.

AUTHOR'S NOTE

Thank you so much for coming back to the Darvel Systems to join me for another tale, this one albeit shorter than most. For the Halloween season, I've felt inclined to do a bunch of shorter pieces and with this one (admittedly inspired by a bit of art of a woman in a frog costume) I was intrigued with the idea of the heroine being transformed into something that she wasn't and having to learn this new life. So, this tale of the Frog Prince does not have a prince transformed into a frog but the heroine, while still containing elements of the original story (her golden ball and his retrieval of it and her acceptance of what fate offered her. It is a sweet little intersection with Darvel compared to the heavier stories and I may write more at times just for something sweet and fun that is also a bit insta-mate-ish.

Happy Reading!

SJ Sanders

ABOUT THE AUTHOR

S.J. Sanders is an author of fantasy, paranormal and sci-fi romance living in central Florida. She has a BA degree in History with a minor in Lit and enjoys reading romance, mythology, ancient history and religions, as well as sculpting and painting in her down time. As a writer, her interest in how cultures diversify and what they would look like on extraterrestrial and other-worldly platforms to the humans interacting with them and finding love fascinates her and inspires much of her work. She loves to challenge reader to dare to fall in love with unusual heroes at every opportunity.

Readers can follow her on Facebook https://www.facebook.com/authorsjsanders
Or join her Facebook group S.J. Sanders Unusual Playhouse
https://www.facebook.com/groups/361374411254067/

Newsletter: https://mailchi.mp/7144ec4ca0e4/sjsandersromance
Twitter:@monsterlyluv
TikTok:@authorsjsanders
Website: https://sjsandersromance.wordpress.com/

Printed in Great Britain
by Amazon